If I had lived in Jesus' time

Peter Graystone

Illustrated by Jacqui Thomas

ABINGDON PRESS

Nashville

How to use this book
A note to all those who will read the book with children.

This book is designed to help children understand what it was like to be a child in Jesus' time. Each right hand page has a picture of a child's everyday life in a small town today, and each left hand page shows equivalent activities taking place in a small town in Palestine in the first century AD. The text, which you should read to the children, applies to both pictures.

As you turn the pages of the book you will find questions. You can use these to help children look at and understand both pictures. To get maximum enjoyment and value from the book, draw children's attention to things which have not changed at all since Jesus was a child (for example, the need to eat, sleep and learn), things which we rely on, but Jesus would not have known (for instance, electrical equipment), and things which Jesus would have experienced but are not now part of most children's experience (such as a clearly defined sense of what it was right and wrong for women to do).

At the back of the book you will find fold-out pages of background information to help you know what to point out from the pictures of Bible times.

Last night I had
a dream. I dreamed that
I was alive hundreds of
years ago – when Jesus
was growing up in
Nazareth.

3

My clothes are waiting
by my bed. They are just
right for today's weather –
hot!

4

Can you see
what protects me
from the sun?

5

Aha! That's what I
could hear! Dad has
got up early to do some
work on the roof.

6

Careful, Dad!
  Can you see what
Dad has done to make
sure he stays safe?

7

Today it is my turn to look after the animals. They are in a naughty mood.

8

Do you have any animals in your home?

I have a strict teacher
who makes me work
hard at school, but
it is too hot today

10

to think about
writing.

How many girls can
you see in each class?

11

My sister is not at
school. I think she
wants to go, but she
is not able to.

12

What do you
think Mom is saying
to my sister?

13

It's a long walk home from school. I can't wait until I'm old enough to ride instead!

How many different
kinds of transportation
can you see?

15

Today is wash day.
Washing clothes is always
easier if you have

someone to help you.
Can you see what
Dad is doing?

My mother always enjoys
shopping. I think she may
have got a bargain!

18

Which pair of shoes
would you choose?

19

After school I love to play
games with my friends.
My aim is getting better
all the time.

Do you play any
of these games?

Music is really important
to everyone in our family.
It makes Grandad laugh

to see my baby brother
try to dance.
Can you see the cymbals?

23

The whole family has gathered together for a meal today because it is

a special occasion.
   What have you had
to eat today?

Before we go to bed,
Dad tells us stories of
men and women who
followed God through

26

good times and bad
times.
What is your favorite
story?

Tomorrow is a special day. It is the day we gather to worship God. When I am grown up I want to stand next to

Dad and sing to God
as loudly as he does.
What would you like
to thank God for today?

For Ruth and Ben

With grateful thanks to Alan Gilliam of
the Church's Ministry Among the Jews for
information and advice on life and customs
in Bible times.

If I had lived in Jesus' time
© 1995 Scripture Union
Text copyright © 1995 Peter Graystone
Illustrations copyright © 1995 Jacqui Thomas

Published in the USA by Abingdon Press, 1995
First published in the UK by Scripture Union, 1995

ISBN 0-687-004381

95 96 97 98 99 00 01 02 03 04 – 10 9 8 7 6 5 4 3 2

Printed and bound in Singapore

wagon as easily as they can pull a plough. They work in pairs when they pull heavy loads and are kept together by a piece of wood called a yoke so they pull in the same direction. A donkey can travel along a muddy, winding track, but carts pulled by oxen or horses need straight roads. The Romans, who governed Nazareth and all the lands around it, were famous for road-building.

Page 16

Washing clothes is done by all the women of the village together in the river, wetting the clothes and then beating them against rocks. The men work in the fields or vineyards and do not play any part at all in the work that needs doing around the house.

Page 18

Travelling merchants bring goods with them to the smaller towns. The shoes do not have a price tag on them. Instead the merchant and the customer spend several minutes agreeing together on what is a fair price. There are very strict rules for shopkeepers which mean that they cannot cheat their customers. For example, if you buy a kilogram of flour they must give you a kilogram and a little bit extra.

Page 20

Some games have been played for thousands of years – games of catching, slinging stones at targets, hide and seek, tug of war, and 'make-believe' games with dolls or acting. There is, though, no evidence of anyone playing football!

Page 22

A party is going on in which all the entertainment is home-made. Many people learn to play music – stringed instruments, wind instruments, and percussion. The cymbals were similar to those still in use in orchestras today. Dancing is popular too, particularly circle dances where everyone follows the same steps.

Page 24

Meals are eaten reclining around a mat on the floor (or, if you are rich, a low table) on which all the food is placed. Usually you do not have a plate – instead you have a piece of flat bread, from which you break a piece and dip it into a large, shared dish of sauce in the middle. There are rules about some foods which may not be eaten – for instance, any food that comes from a pig, such as sausages or ham or bacon. Here, though, you can see a very special once-yearly meal called the Passover. During this meal, the father tells the

thrilling story of how the family's ancestors escaped from a cruel king of Egypt. Every type of food eaten during the meal – lamb, flat bread, bitter herbs, wine – reminds them of a particular part of the story.

Page 26

Not very many people were able to read and write (virtually no women at all and only a small number of men, called scribes, who were responsible for explaining the laws in what we now call the Old Testament and making hand-written copies of them with precise care). However, for hundreds of years there was a tradition of stories of the great men and women of faith being passed on by word of mouth from parent to child.

Page 28

Only men over the age of thirteen are able to take part in the service. They sit in the main part of the synagogue where they join in the singing and say prayers. Sometimes they may be asked to read a part of what we now call the Old Testament. They stand up out of respect when they are reading God's word, but sit down when they are saying words of their own. Women and children do not take an active part – they may only watch from a gallery or separate area at the side.

Here is some more information on the pictures of life in Jesus' time

Page 3
The bed is a thin mattress on the floor, which can be rolled up out of the way during the day. All the family sleeps together on the same mat, with their cloaks spread over them. With so many people living in just one room, there isn't space for everyone to have a bed. And anyway, it is warmer at night!

Page 4
The boy is wearing a cotton tunic – a simple piece of material folded in the middle and sewn up the sides. When he was younger he would have run around naked, and when he is older he will wear a belt to hold the tunic at the waist and a cloak on top of it. He has leather sandals for his feet. The square of material is for his head – folded into a triangle and secured with a piece of cord. When the sun is at its hottest this is vital protection, but in a gale he can wrap it round his face to keep out the hail or the dust as well.

Page 6
The roof of the house is flat, and you can get onto it by walking up the stairs at the side of the house. By law, builders have to put a parapet round the edge to stop people falling off. It is used for storage, or for laying out crops or clothes to dry in the sun. In summer, it is possible to build a temporary extension on the roof out of branches – particularly useful when guests come to stay!

Page 8
At night the family shares the house with animals. These are not pets, but animals such as goats and chickens which are needed for food. The animals are eating out of a wooden manger, which doubles up as a bed when a baby is born! The raised section of the room means that the humans can at least eat and sleep without animals walking all over them – but it doesn't keep out the insects or the smoke from the fire!

Page 10
Only boys go to school – they start at the age of five. Their class is in one of the rooms of the synagogue. The boys have to sit in absolutely straight lines in front of the teacher – in fact they nickname the classroom 'the vineyard'. Their teacher (called 'rabbi') is very strict, and if they slack or wriggle out of line he has a big stick to use to regain their attention! However, the teacher is also under instructions to be kind – he could lose his job if he is too harsh. Most of the lessons are learning sentences from the Jewish Law (now part of the Old Testament) by heart. They repeat them over and over again, rocking backwards and forwards so that the rhythm helps the words stick in their memories.

Page 12
The girls do not go to school, but that does not mean they are not learning. In the home their mothers teach them to spin, sew, cook and clean.

Page 14
The donkey is the poor family's basic form of transport. Oxen are used in many ways by farmers, since they can pull a